THE
FORGOTTEN
BEAR

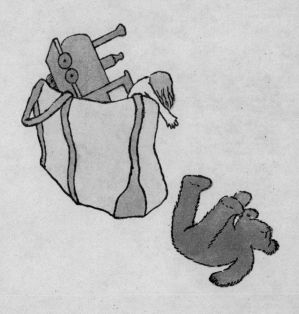

THE FORGOTTEN BEAR

by
Consuelo Joerns

SCHOLASTIC BOOK SERVICES
NEW YORK • TORONTO • LONDON • AUCKLAND • SYDNEY • TOKYO

ISBN: 0-590-12103-0

13 12 11 10 9 8 7 6 5 4 3 2   0 1 2 3 4/8

Printed in the U. S. A.   11

For Kreekus

S am was a forgotten bear,
left behind by mistake in the attic

of an old summerhouse on a very small island.

Years passed. He was very lonely and brooded a great deal.

Sometimes he watched at the window for a
boat that might take him away. Ships passed
by but none came to the island.

One day Sam opened an old chest in the attic
to see what was inside.

He found a big bundle marked **FIRECRACKERS**,
which was almost too heavy to lift, and
a bottle that had something inside it.

to be
rescued—
put a note
in this bottle
and put it
out to sea
Peter

Inside the bottle was a message signed, "Peter."

Sam wrote a note to Peter and put it in the
bottle. Then he carefully put back the cork

and tossed the bottle out of the window. He watched it bobbing on the waves until it was out of sight.

Every day Sam listened at the attic door
for the sound of Peter's footsteps.

And every day he watched at the window,
hoping to see Peter arrive in a boat.

He had almost given up hope when one day
Sam heard footsteps coming upstairs!

Then the attic door opened and in walked
a boy — carrying Sam's note.

"I'm Peter," he said. "Are you Sam Bear?"
It was a grand meeting.

"We'll put your chest in the sailboat," said Peter, "and leave right away."

And down the stairs they went, bumping
the chest between them.

They sailed very fast and the house got
smaller and smaller. "Look," said Peter,
"there's Captain John's boat." And he
pointed to a ship with three sails.

Now they were out
so far the house
looked like a speck
in the distance.

Suddenly dark clouds formed overhead.
The waves got higher and higher.

The wind almost blew the sailboat over.
"Hang on!" shouted Peter, who was having
a very difficult time hanging on himself.

Just then there was a flash of lightning
and it struck the old chest.

For a moment everything was black—

Then all at once the firecrackers went off
and filled the sky with brilliant lights and
even a portrait of George Washington.

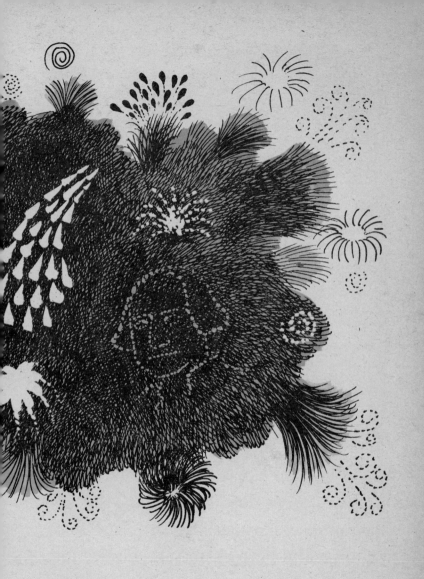

"Good heavens!" cried Captain John when he saw George Washington in the sky and then more explosions. "What's that?" and he turned his boat around and headed for the lights. "You never can tell," he told his mate, "it might be a distress signal!"

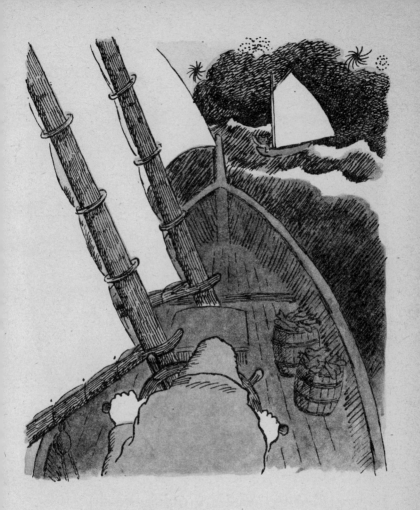

When Captain John came nearer he saw
Peter's small sailboat rocking on the
waves. "AHOY, PETER!" he shouted.
"We'll have you aboard in a jiffy!"

They pulled Peter and Sam aboard and
fastened the sailboat to a towrope.
"Wheeew! what a narrow escape, my lad,"
said Captain John. "Now go below till
your teeth stop chattering."

Captain John gave them some hot tea.
"Where'd you get those signals?" he asked.
"The mate and I have never seen anything
like it! And who's your friend here?"

"This is Sam," said Peter proudly,
"and the signals must have been in his chest!"
"What a clever bear," said Captain John.
"You ought never to go sailing without him."

And with that he put a very special hat
on Sam.

And afterward Sam always went sailing
with Peter.